Father Joe's Six Golden Seeds

SPECIAL EDITION

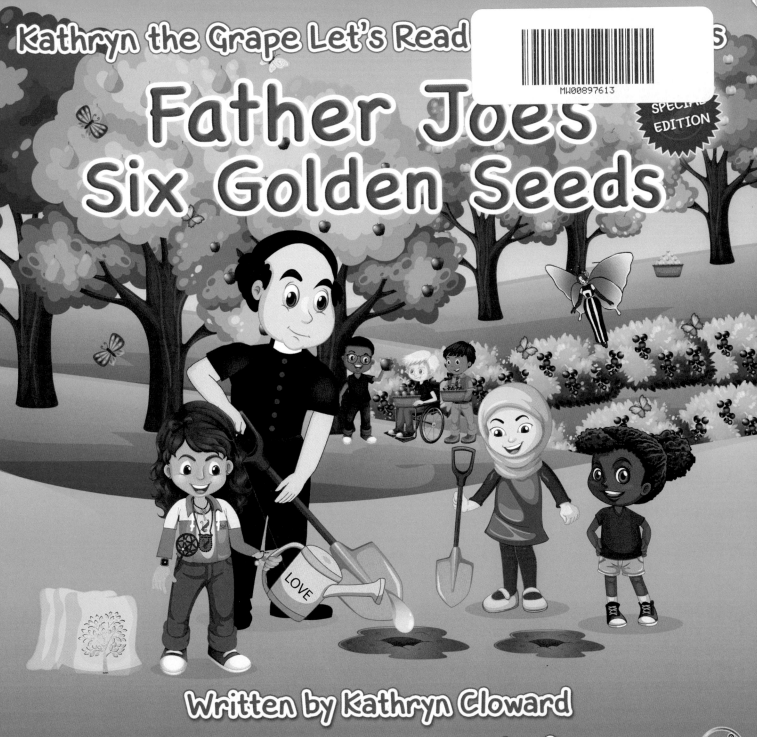

Written by Kathryn Cloward

Illustrated by Aneeza Ashraf

Kathryn the Grape Let's Read Together Series

Father Joe's Six Golden Seeds
is published and distributed by Kandon Unlimited, Inc.

Text and Illustrations Copyright
© 2021 Kathryn Cloward and Kandon Unlimited, Inc.

Kathryn the Grape® and Father Joe's Six Golden Seeds®
are registered trademarks of Kandon Unlimited, Inc.
All characters, images, and concepts related to Kathryn the Grape and
Father Joe's Six Golden Seeds are the sole property of Kandon Unlimited, Inc.

All rights reserved.

No part of this book may be used or reproduced in any manner whatsoever
without written permission from Kandon Unlimited, Inc., except in the case of brief
quotations embodied in critical articles and reviews.

Library of Congress Number: 2020935533

ISBN-13: 978-0-991290598
ISBN-10: 0991290593

Cover and interior layout designed by David Stone.

This book was created with love for everyone to enjoy together.

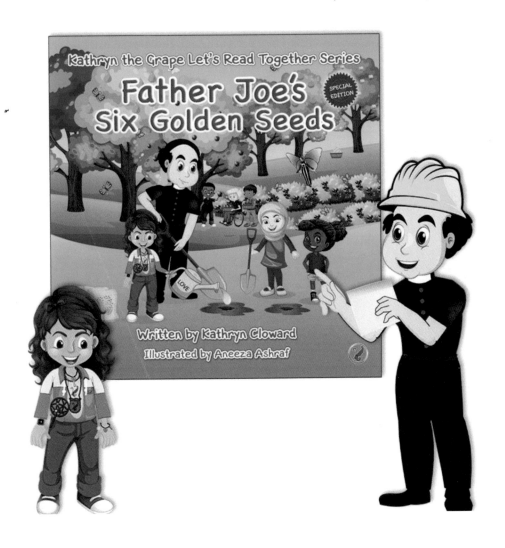

This is Father Joe. He's a good man. He helps others in any way he can.

My mom works with Father Joe at a charity every day. They help people have food and clothes, and a place to stay.

Mom bought my favorite outfit from the charity's thrift store. Donated items are sold to raise money to help others more.

Whenever I visit my mom at work, Father Joe has jobs for me to complete.
I make sandwiches and send letters. Sometimes I pick up trash in the street.

In downtown where there once was a big empty space, Father Joe was tasked to build a homeless shelter in its place.

At first many people couldn't understand the whole vision he saw in his mind. But he knew his purpose, and that it would all get built in time.

A Boy Scout for life,
Father Joe honored his
calling every day.
To *be prepared* and
help others at all times
is the scouting way.

His life's story is like a garden that's rooted by simple seeds. His purpose has always been clear — to help our neighbors in need.

A humble man who's had great impact, that's our friend Father Joe. His message of goodness is simple for everyone in the world to know.

Our friend Father Joe helps people grow. He built a housing community for neighbors in need.

One thing he'll always say
is that everyone matters
the same. He's taught us
how to be with his
Six Golden Seeds.

Always be compassionate to everyone including yourself.

Forgive easily
and forget all else.

Respect your neighbor.
(Everyone is our neighbor.)

Help your neighbor.
(Everyone is our neighbor.)

Empower yourself and others to earn the way.

Experience God in everything and everyone every day.

Our friend Father Joe has inspired us to know life is like planting seeds. Love is water everyone needs.

Sometimes we will disagree. But we can still live peacefully.

Let's be kind
and plant goodness.
Grow our Six Golden Seeds
to fullness.

Always be compassionate to everyone including yourself.

Forgive easily
and forget all else.

Respect your neighbor.
(Everyone is our neighbor.)

Help your neighbor.
(Everyone is our neighbor.)

Empower yourself and others to earn the way.

Experience God in everything and everyone every day.

No matter your age or where you live, everyone has something to give.

Pass along these
Six Golden Seeds.
Let's grow in unity.

Father Joe's Six Golden Seeds

**Always be compassionate
to everyone including yourself.**

Forgive easily and forget all else.

Respect your neighbor.

Help your neighbor.

**Empower yourself and others
to earn the way.**

**Experience God in everything
and everyone every day.**

A Message From Father Joe

Thank you for reading my story. It makes me feel happy knowing that you now have these Six Golden Seeds for yourself. May you live them throughout your life. Experience God's goodness always by remembering to be compassionate, forgiving, respectful, helpful, and empowering.

God Bless,

Father Joe

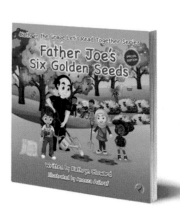

Book for Youth

Book for Teens & Adults

A portion of book proceeds
will benefit children in need.

Hi! My name is Kathryn the Grape.

Purple is my favorite color and I wear it every day.

When I was a little girl, I loved to write songs and sing them to my dolls. I dreamed about one day sharing my songs with people.

My mom loved to read. Every night before I went to sleep, she read stories to me. It was my favorite part of the day.

Many years later, my mom suggested sharing Kathryn the Grape stories with other people. I thought it was a great idea! Now you can read and sing along with me as we grow through life.

Your friend,
Kathryn the Grape

Let's be friends and grow up together!

Kathryn the Grape
Let's Read Together Series

Kathryn the Grape
Affirmation Series

Kathryn the Grape
YouTube Series

Listen at KathryntheGrape.com

YouTube

Apple Music

Spotify

Amazon Music

YouTube Music

Kathryn the Grape Let's Read Together Series

Kathryn the Grape Affirmation Series

I am magical.

I am colorful.

I am love.

I am kind.

I am unique.

I am grateful.

I am joyful.

Kathryn the Grape Affirmation Series
COLORING BOOKS

I am magical.

I am colorful.

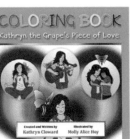

I am love.

I am kind.

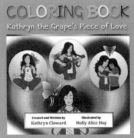

I am unique.

I am grateful.

I am joyful.

"Let's choose to ripple love. Let peace be our energy."

Did you enjoy reading this book?

It would be greatly appreciated if you'd write and share an honest review of this book on Amazon.

Made in the USA
Las Vegas, NV
21 July 2021

26807016R20043